CARDINAL
MEDIA

Max's Bright Smile
Text Copyright © Qi Zhi
Illustration Copyright © Cheng Yue
Edited by Marie Kruegel
English Copyright © 2018 by Cardinal Media, LLC.
ISBN 978-1-64074-011-2
Through Jiangsu Phoenix Education Publishing Ltd.
All rights reserved. No part of this publication may be reproduced,
stored in a retrieval system, or transmitted in any form or by any means,
electronic, mechanical, photocopying, recording or otherwise,
without the prior permission of the publishers.
Printed in China
2 4 6 8 10 9 7 5 3 1

Max's Bright Smile

Written by Qi Zhi
Illustrated by Cheng Yue

CARDINAL
MEDIA

Max was a little black
cat who lived on the
corner of the street.

One night it was
as dark outside
as Max's fur.

A goose couldn't find her way home.

A pig couldn't find
the door of his house.

Max squatted in the darkness, worried.

"Goodness! I cannot see the road," an old granny murmured while walking.

A little girl ran by, calling,
"Mom, Mom! I'm scared!"

"What can I do for them?" Max
wondered as he sat in the darkness.

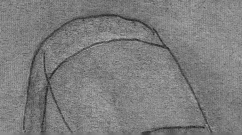

Max went inside and looked into the mirror. He was as dark as the night.

Max grinned at himself.

Max noticed that although he was black, his teeth were white.

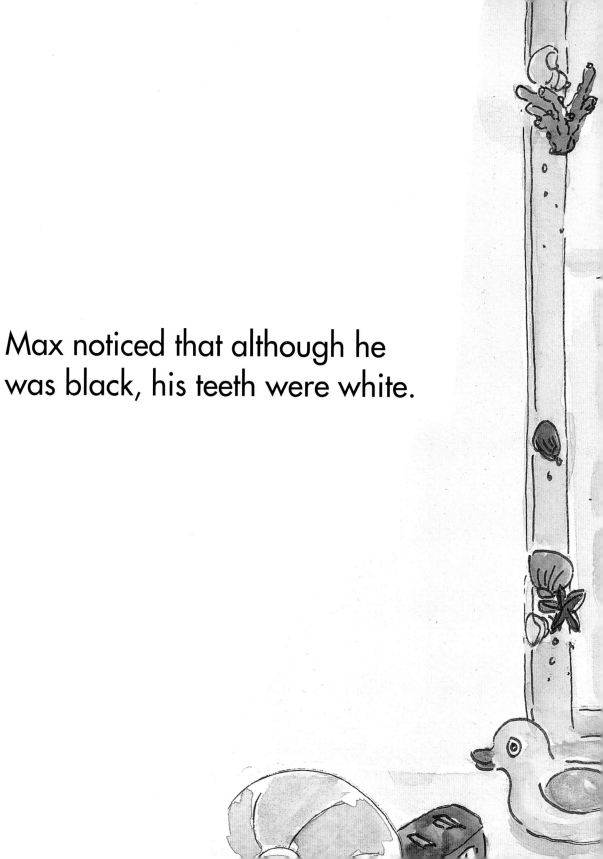

Max had an idea.

He began to brush his teeth.

Max brushed and brushed.

He brushed his teeth so they were as white as daylight.

He sat outside and
flashed his bright grin,
lighting up the darkness.

The pig and the goose passed by happily.

Max was happy. His bright smile had helped his friends.